S0-BSX-549

S0-BSX-549

Michelle

Best Wishes

Jim Poulter

UNCLE BANJO'S NETT-NETT STORIES

by Jim Poulter

illustrated by John Fairbridge

RED HEN

First published 1994
RED HEN ENTERPRISES
278 Serpells Rd
Templestowe 3106
Victoria Australia
ph (03) 842 3598
fax (03) 842 8665
Copyright © Jim Poulter 1994

This book is copyright, apart from any fair dealings for the
purpose of private study, research, criticism, or review, as
permitted under the Copyright Act. No part may be reproduced
by any person without written permission. Inquiries may be
directed to the publisher.

National Library of Australia
Cataloguing-in-Publication Data

Poulter, Jim
   Uncle Banjo's Nett-Nett Stories
   ISBN 0 949196 07 X

   I — Fairbridge, John. 11. Title

A823.3

Produced by Island Graphics Pty Ltd
Typset by Solo Typesetting, South Australia
Printed in Singapore

ABOUT THE AUTHOR

Jim Poulter was born in 1941 and is married to Barbara. They
have three adult children and a grandchild. Jim comes from a
family with a strong tradition of storytelling. He has also
continued his family's tradition, begun in 1840, of strong
association with the Aboriginal community. Many of Jim's
books are Aboriginal in theme, reflecting this family heritage.
It also reflects Jim's personal ambition to help strengthen
recognition of the vital way in which Aboriginal language,
humour, values and perceptions, can continue to help shape
our national culture and character.

**Dedicated to Banjo Clarke
and his sons Len and Ian**

For all they have shared with me over the years

Banjo (Henry) Clarke, born in 1922 is Senior Elder of the Gunditjmara tribe, Kirrae Clan in the Western District of Victoria. His tribe has always been known, for extremely good reasons, as "The Fighting Gunditjmara". His tribe has in fact produced every Victorian Aboriginal boxing champion, of which Banjo was one. Banjo is also the hereditary Keeper of Framlingham Forest. His house overlooks the Hopkin's river rapids, at the edge of the forest, which is his Dreaming place. This book is intended as a tribute to both the person and his Dreaming.

ABOUT THIS BOOK

Uncle Banjo is an old Aboriginal man I have known for a long while and, as I have got to know him, he has trusted me with more and more of his stories.

A few years ago, Uncle Banjo asked me if I knew about Nett-Netts. I had heard a little bit about them and knew that very few people have ever seen Nett-Netts except for old Aboriginal people like Uncle Banjo, whom the Nett-Netts have grown to trust.

Nett-Netts are like little Aboriginal elves and are about the size of a two or three year old child. They are magic little people who can turn themselves into shadows and become invisible by being part of another shadow. Even if you were out in the desert, a Nett-Nett could still follow you, by moving from rock shadow to rock shadow, or even by being part of your own shadow.

Uncle Banjo has always lived right next to Framlingham Forest. He often sits quietly by himself on a log or a stump, deep in the shady greenness of the forest. He listens to the birds, watches the animals, and talks to them as everyday friends.

But Banjo also knew that there were other beings who quietly watched him from the shadows. Beings that were still too shy to come out into the open with him, as all the forest animals had learned to do.

Finally, after Uncle Banjo had been coming to the forest like this for more than fifty years, the Netts-Netts came out from the shadows to meet him. So now they will sit with old Uncle Banjo deep in the Framlingham Forest and tell him their stories.

Nett-Netts are part of the force for good in this world and their job is to protect children. So they follow children around, flitting from shadow to shadow, trying to protect them from harm—especially from the nasty mischief of Mee-Mees, who are their sworn enemies.

Sometimes, when you are walking through the Australian bush, if you stop suddenly, you might hear the sound of the Nett-Nett's footstep, stopping after yours. Now, some people will try to say that this is only an echo. But what is an echo? Aboriginal people will tell you that sometimes, the Nett-Netts will only seem to be like an echo or a shadow. But that does not mean that Nett-Netts are not real.

When Uncle Banjo told me these things, it all made sense. I mean, have you ever had the feeling you were being followed, but when you turned around nobody was there? Well it might have been a Nett-Nett. Have you ever seen a shadow next to a tree or a bush, that you thought was somebody, but when you looked closer it was nobody? Well it might have been a Nett-Nett.

Uncle Banjo told me that Nett-Netts are the shadows of children's spirits that became separated from their spirit child in the Dreamtime. So the Nett-Netts made their way into the real world, to wait until the child they belonged to was born. But then I learned something even more amazing. About 150 years ago the Nett-Netts joined an international organisation of magic little folk, like leprechauns, elves, fairies, and pixies. Together, all the magic little folk of the world helped to bring Father Christmas into being!

So nowadays, as well as having their ordinary day-to-day job of protecting children, Nett-Netts also have another special job to do just before Christmas.

As members of their international organisation of magic little folk, the Nett-Netts have to keep an updated list of all the babies being born in Australia, and of all the kids who have changed their address since the last Christmas. This is so that Santa can bring presents to each child for Christmas.

This really zapped me, and Uncle Banjo's eyes twinkled as I looked at him with my mouth open. But when I thought about it, it all fitted together, just like everything else Uncle Banjo has ever told me. After all, Father Christmas had never been heard of until about 150 years ago. But we know he has something to do with the spirit of St Nicholas, who had lived about one thousand six hundred years ago.

Then, when Uncle Banjo saw that I understood, he told me the stories about how the Nett-Netts had twice saved Christmas from being wrecked. The first time was when there was trouble with the reindeer not wanting to come to Australia because of the hot weather. The second time, was when the Nett-Netts discoverd a plot by their arch enemies, the nasty Mee-Mees, to kidnap Santa.

Now, you might not have heard of the Mee-Mees before, but they are in fact part of the force for evil in this world. They belong to an opposing international organisation of Bad Little Folk. Goblins, Gremlins, Imps, Trolls and whatnot. The thing that Mee-Mees love more than anything is hearing children cry. They snigger and giggle with glee. But when children laugh, boy, does that give them the irrits.

But perhaps I had better let you get on with reading the stories for yourself. This book has four stories in it. The first is the Dreamtime story of how Nett-Netts came to be. The second is the story of how Santa Claus came to be. The third is the story of how the hole in the ozone nearly wrecked Christmas, and the last story is about the B.L.F. (standing, of course, for Bad Little Folk) and how they tried to wreck Christmas.

I hope you enjoy the stories and learn something new about the magic little folk we have in Australia.

THE NETT-NETT DREAMTIME STORY

A long long time ago, the world was formed in a Dream by the Spirit of All Life. God liked the Dream and did not want the Dream to end. So God sent life into the Dream to make it real and entrusted mankind with the secret of how to Dream. To make sure that these Dreaming secrets could be safely passed on to future generations, God created the spirits of all children ever to be born.

And so it is that the spirits of all unborn children must wait in the Dreamtime, until it is their turn to be born.

Children cannot be born until their spirits are found in a dream by their fathers, and told how to find the body of their mother, who will make their flesh. For it is only as beings of flesh and blood that children can enter the real world.

But long, long ago when the first fathers began their dreaming, the spirit children were afraid of making the journey from the Dreamtime to their mother's body. They were afraid of the sadness and pain in the real world.

In the Dreamtime there was no hunger, pain or sadness. It was a warm and happy place that the spirit children all liked, and they wanted to keep their friendships with each other. So the spirit children hid from the dreaming search of their fathers and did not answer their calls.

But soon the children could feel the tears of their mothers and the sorrow of their fathers. Then they knew that the world needed the laughter of children. They too, could see that without children, the secret of Dreaming would not be passed on, and the Earth would have no Caretakers.

For the first time the spirit children were unhappy. They did not know what to do because they were still too frightened to make the journey. But while they were all sitting around unhappily, one of the spirit children chanced to see her spirit shadow. For just as we have shadows in the real world, so did the spirit children have their spirit shadows, which they called Nett-Netts.

So when she saw her Nett-Nett, the spirit child had an idea. The idea was that the spirit children would share their life force with their shadows. Then, as each child was called by their father in a dream, to make the journey to the body of their mother, they would leave their Nett-Nett behind in the Dreaming.

If the child then found after they were born, that the world was safe, they would call their Nett-Nett to join them in the real world. If they found that the world was unsafe, the Nett-Nett would recall the child's spirit to the Dreamtime, and no more children would be born into the real world.

All the spirit children in the Dreamtime agreed with the plan, and one by one spirit children left the Dreaming, in answer to the dreaming call of their fathers.

But their plan went wrong.

When life had been sent into the first Dreaming to continue the creation work and allow the Spirit of Life to rest, one Creator Spirit had later kept their Dreamtime powers. All the other Creator Spirits had surrendered their Dreamtime powers once the creation work was finished, and they became a creature or landmark we see today. All of the Creator Spirits that is, except for the Mook-Mook.

The Mook-Mook was a Creator Spirit whose gift to the world was chance and change, rather than a thing we can see and feel. The Mook-Mook therefore was, and still remains today, a spirit of mischief. A spirit with the power to change our lives, as if by fortune or misfortune.

And so the Mook-Mook wrought his mischief on the spirit children. When they were born into the real world, the spirit children did not remember their Dreamtime lives. Because of the Mook-Mook's mischief, the children forgot about their Nett-Netts, and the promise they had made to call their Nett-Netts into the real world.

Time went by, and the Nett-Netts at last realised they had been forgotten by their soul mates. So the Nett-Netts decided to find their own way into the real world and seek out the children to whom they belonged.

Even the Nett-Netts of the children still to be born decided to leave the Dreamtime, each promising to wait in the real world until their spirit partner was born, when they would then be re-united.

So all the Nett-Netts left the Dreamtime, expecting to follow a Dreamtime Pathway to the real world. But no complete pathway remained. The nearest they could get to the real world was the Dreaming Place of the Mook-Mook. This was a place called Mookedah, and it exists on the edge of reality.

When the despairing Nett-Netts found that they could not make the final journey to the real world, and that they were trapped in Mookedah, they began to cry. And their sorrow filled all of time.

In a Dream, an old Gadaidja Man heard the crying of the trapped Nett-Netts, and began chanting a spell to bridge their journey to the real world.

The Gadaidja Man's powerful Dreaming Spell reached Mookedah, and for a time opened a pathway into the real world. In doing this, thousands of Nett-Netts were able to take the final step from Mookedah to the real world, before the pathway closed once again.

Once in the real world each Nett-Nett who had escaped from Mookedah was at last, able to search for the child to whom they belonged and to be reunited with them.

The Mook-Mook was in fact relieved to see this happen for, although it is mischievious, the Mook-Mook does not intend harm to come from its tricks.

So the Mook-Mook told the rest of the Nett-Netts, who had not been called, that a Dreamtime Pathway to the real world would open for any Nett-Nett called by a child before that child's twelfth birthday.

It is at this age that childhood ends and one begins taking up the responsibilities of adulthood. Not all adult responsibilities can be known at twelve; but the first responsibility of all human beings must be known before childhood ends. And this first responsibility is to care for the earth.

The calling of one's Nett-Nett therefore happens by the child knowing their responsibility to the environment. Each child must understand that the first job of every human being, is to be a Caretaker of the Earth. The child's acceptance of their responsibilities to the earth will irrisistably attract their Nett-Nett to wherever the child is.

And once your Nett-Nett finds you, your life forces are once more united. You are at peace with yourself and the world because you are a whole person once more, and you know that your first job is to protect all life on earth.

THE GREAT MEETING
OF MAGIC LITTLE FOLK

When the Nett-Netts arrived in the real world, they had no idea when the children that they belonged to would be born. It could be the next day or in a thousand years.

They had no way of finding their children, apart from the sort of magnetism that exists between the Nett-Nett and their child. Many Nett-Netts did not succeed in finding their child, particularly when the magnetism was weakened by the child not knowing their responsibilities to protect the environment.

So all the Nett-Netts finally had a meeting to decide what to do. The answer to their problem was simple. They all agreed. Seeing they did not know when their child would be born, or even if they would be able to find their child when it was born, they would try as best they could to protect all children.

And the Nett-Netts could see that they had a lot of work to do. Not only in Australia, but all around the world, too many children were sad and unsafe. The children of the world seemed to have too little joy or magic in their lives. Other magic little folk from all around the world also saw the sadness of the children and were greatly concerned.

Elves, Leprechauns, Fairies, Sprites, Brownies, Pixies and all the other magic little folk of the world were so concerned with the happiness and safety of children, that a huge International Meeting of Good Little Folk was called, to be held in a gigantic cave, somewhere in the misty greenness of Ireland.

Fortunately, a young Leprechaun, Shamus, who was less than five hundred years old, had decided to emigrate from Ireland to Australia. Shamus happened to meet the Nett-Netts and arranged for them to send representatives to this international convention. With great excitement and pleasure, the Nett-Netts elected two of them, Angie and Neville, to represent Australia. Arrangements were then made to magically transport Angie and Neville from Australia all the way to Ireland.

On the appointed day, at the appointed hour, Neville and Angie held hands tightly. Through the combined magic of all the good little folk in the world, the two Nett-Netts suddenly found themselves transported in the blinking of an eye, into the middle of the huge Irish cavern.

Angie and Neville stared round in amazement at the flickering torchlit scene. Hundreds of magic little folk from countries around the world were all gathered there in their traditional costumes. Luckily, Angie and Neville had worn their traditional red lap-laps, feather shoes and headbands, but normally they just wore tee shirt and jeans.

The two Nett-Netts could see that most other magic folk were about their size, and that was about the same size as a two or three year old child. But some of the others, like fairies and sprites, were much smaller.

It was all colour, movement and excitement, with a constant babble of discussion going on, until an important looking Elf stood on the platform at the front. He adjusted his pointed yellow elf hat, banged his wooden hammer on the desk, and called for quiet.

"Order, order!"

Gradually the babble subsided. The Presiding Elf gave an "Erherhrrmff" and then began a welcoming speech.

"The heartiest of welcomes one and all, to this the First Annual Meeting of our esteemed international co-ordinating body, which it has been proposed, we call Elves and Little Folk International Network. Or as we would call it for short, E.L.F.I.N."

"Is the meeting in favour of this name?"

Wild clapping and cheering broke out in answer to the question. The Presiding Elf smiled broadly, and declared the motion carried by acclamation. He then held up his hands for silence.

"Thank you indeed for your attendance. Many of you have come great distances from all over the world to be here tonight, and even with the help of our combined magic it is still no easy task. Now I would like to call on our Irish members to give a special welcome to the newest magic little folk to join our international network. Thank you Finnegan."

To generous applause, a green suited leprechaun seated in the audience rose. He stepped to the front near the Presiding Elf's desk and smiled broadly.

"Ah, thank you to be sure Mr Presiding Elf, or Pomp, as we all know and love you. Ah yes, it is indeed, indeed a great personal pleasure for myself to be making the official welcome to our newest members from Australia. This is because it was my own nephew Shamus, a fine young fellow, who first made contact with our new members the Nett-Netts, and he encouraged them to attend this meeting, that he did."

Finnegan stopped and indicated to Shamus with a sweep of his hand. The audience again clapped as the green suited Shamus briefly rose from his seat, nodded shyly and sat down again. Finnegan then continued.

"Ah to be sure young Shamus is only a stripling youth of 453 years of age, and for reasons we won't talk about right now, he travelled all the way to Australia. There he became firm friends with our two guests here tonight. Ladies and gentlemen please extend a fine and warm welcome to our Nett-Nett friends all the way from Australia to be sure, Angie and Neville."

Enthusiastic clapping broke out in the crowded cavern. Slowly, and with a bit of prompting from Shamus who was sitting next to them, two dark-skinned little folk stood up and nodded to the applauding audience. Both Neville and Angie's chubby little faces beamed with shy smiles.

"Thank you Finnegan for those fine words," said Pomp from the table at the front.

"Now without further ado, you all know why we are here. We need to figure out how to make sure that the children of the world are safer and happier than they are now."

There were lots of "Here, here!" comments, murmurs of approval and nods of agreement, so Pomp called for ideas and suggestions.

Lots of little folk then told various stories and things they had seen about how unhappy children were, but unfortunately, nobody came up with ideas. The conversation just went around in circles for a couple of hours, and everybody was getting a bit frustrated.

Finally, an Elf who was nearly two thousand years old, remembered that when he was young he had helped a saintly old man take presents to children at Christmas time.

"Yes, I remember now. His name was Nicholas. After he died he was made a Saint. Saint Nicholas, that was him. I tell you he really knew how to make children happy. It's a pity we couldn't get some advice from him. I reckon he would know what to do."

Pomp's eyes gleamed and he waggled a finger.

"Well now, are we or aren't we magic little folk? If we want the advice of someone like this Saint Nicholas, all we have to do is the right ceremony, the right incantation, the right spell, and hey presto we could talk to the Spirit of Saint Nicholas!"

There was a huge hubbub of excitement at Pomp's comment as little folk exchanged comments.

Of course. Easy as pie. Ask the Spirit of St Nicholas! Couldn't be simpler. The spirit of St Nicholas would surely have some idea how to make children's lives happier.

Pomp bashed his mallet on the table and called for order again.

"Righto, shush up. It seems like we are all in agreement. So clear the centre of the cave, get some magic chalk and draw a five sided star on the floor. Put candles at each point and we will all gather in a circle to start the magic chant."

There was a flurry of activity, and soon all was in readiness. The little folk held hands around the circle and began to chant "Saint Nicholas, Saint Nicholas". More and more, though, their chant became mumbled and began to sound different.

"Saint Nicholas, Saint Nichlas, Sant Niklas, Sant Niklos, Santni Klos, Santna Klos, Santa Klos, Santa Claus . . ."

All this while the Mook-Mook Spirit, who had invisibly followed Neville and Angie to see what they were up to, had been watching from the shadows.

A mischevious glint shone in the Mook-Mook's eyes as it heard the mumbled chant of the magic little folk, and he worked his magic to play his best trick yet.

Instead of the little folk just talking to the spirit of St Nicholas and getting advice, suddenly in the middle of the five pointed star, stood a confused looking old man. He had apple red cheeks, flowing white whiskers, a fur lined red suit, and was as plump as a christmas pudding.

The magic little folk were shocked into silence as they saw the old man stare around blankly at them.

Finally, Pomp spoke.

"Er, excuse me, but who are you, where did you come from and what are you doing here?"

The old man removed his red stocking cap and scratched his silvery hair in a befuddled way.

"Who am I? Well all I know is my name is Santa Claus! Where did I come from? I have not the faintest idea! What am I doing here? Well again, all I can tell you is that it is my job to bring happiness to children at Christmas time. Don't ask me how I know, I just know, and I am going to need all the help I can get."

Well, the rest is history.

Santa Claus became Father Christmas and, with the help of the good little magic folk from around the world, he began the job of bringing happiness at to children at Christmas time. A magic castle and toy factory was created at the North Pole, and from there each year Father Christmas magically brings the toys, made by the elves, to all the children who celebrate Christmas.

But his magic can only work if you believe in him.

HOW THE HOLE IN THE OZONE THREATENED CHRISTMAS

Up at the North Pole, all through the year, Santa's Elves work hard making presents for children. They make lots and lots of toys, and as soon as each toy is finished, it is placed in a magic bag.

Because it is a magic bag, no matter how many toys are put in it, the bag never fills right up. Each elf toymaker has a list of children's names to work to, and a name is crossed off each time a toy is finished and placed in the bag.

So it is very important that Santa's elves have up-to-date lists of children's names, and where they live. The job has, of course, been made a bit easier since computers have been invented, but it is still a huge task.

In this important task of keeping the list of children's names up-to-date, Santa and his elf workers are helped by a special organisation of the world's magic good little folk.

This organisation has been running for about 150 years, and is known as "Elves and Little Folk International Network", or E.L.F.I.N. for short.

Our story really starts just before Christmas only a couple of years ago. All of the toys to be delivered had been finished a bit ahead of schedule, and packed away in the magic bag.

This was always a time of great excitement. The elves felt pleased with a job well done. Santa looked forward to his big night of the year and hummed as he polished his big black boots. Then he checked the travel details with Edwin, his elf foreman.

Santa and Edwin always had things worked out to a tee. The journey would always start in the east from the international date line in the Pacific, late on Christmas Eve. The first countries to be visited were therefore New Zealand and Australia.

Santa would then head west following the night, visiting all the countries that celebrated Christmas. He would then finish up with the U.S.A. and Canada, before dawn on Christmas morning. From Canada, it was, of course, only a short hop home to the North Pole.

The reindeer, too, were looking forward to their big night out for the year, and started to discuss the travel plans.

But this is when things started to go wrong.

The reindeer started talking about the weather. They were used to the snow and ice of the arctic. In fact they loved the cold weather. They found the heat of the countries having summer just a bit hard to handle. New Zealand was, by and large, alright. But when the reindeer started to talk about Australian weather, they got down to some serious grumbling.

I mean, it could get impossibly hot in Australia. It was bad enough in the cities, but in the bush and the outback, fair dinkum, it got so hot that even the lizards wore thongs.

And that wasn't the worst of it. When Penny, the Reindeer Union shop steward, read the forecast for Australia, she was not impressed. Blistering hot! That was what the forecast was! But that wasn't all. There was also some talk about a hole in the Ozone Layer that was letting in buckets of Ultra Violet Radiation and goodness knows what else!

No, it wasn't good enough at all. Penny could clearly see that this hot weather, ozone hole, and U.V. radiation stuff all added up to a significant Occupational Health and Safety risk for her Comrade Reindeer. So Penny called a Stopwork Meeting.

Edwin Elf bustled down to the office where he and Santa worked, mumbling to himself in a worried way. Santa could see the worry lines all across Edwin's face.

"Edwin! What on earth is wrong?"

"Oh trouble, big trouble, Santa. The reindeer have got themselves in an awful gripe about the weather in Australia, and are on the point of going on strike!"

Santa looked at Edwin in shock and horror.

"On strike? But that would wreck Christmas! Children would not get any presents! This is terrible Edwin! What are the reindeer saying? How can we solve this problem?"

Santa was now in just as big a flap as Edwin, who said that they hadn't actually called a strike, but had passed a number of motions about how they felt. Santa eagerly asked Edwin to read the motions to him, so Edwin did.

Motion one. We brother and sister reindeer, hearby deplore and condemn the employment conditions (viz. very hot weather) to be experienced in Australia this year, and are especially concerned as to the possible Ultra-Violet health dangers associated with the hole in the ozone layer.

Motion two. We the Federated Union of Christmas Reindeer (North Pole Chapter) unanimously consider the Australian weather conditions (including ozone layer hole and associated Ultra-Violet radiation) to constitute an unacceptable risk to Occupational Health and Safety.

Motion three. We the aforementioned reindeer, call on our employer, Father Christmas and his delegated elves, to enter into meaningful negotiations, to redress the effect of unfair, oppressive and exploitive weather conditions applying to reindeer in the Australian continental area.

On hearing this, Santa put his hand on his chin and stroked his silvery beard with worry.

"You're right Edwin. They haven't gone on strike yet, but unless we do something to overcome this Australian weather problem, the reindeer will go on strike for sure. If that happens, then Christmas will be wrecked for all the children in the world. This is certainly not a situation to ho ho ho about."

Then Edwin had an idea. He suggested that maybe they should check the Reindeer's Award, to see just what it did say about their working conditions. Santa agreed that this was a good move, and Edwin immediately searched a filing cabinet.

As soon as he found the document, Santa and Edwin looked at it together. Edwin pointed to the appropriate clause in the award and read it out aloud.

"The aforesaid reindeer, for agreed recompense of hay and warm stables, shall assist delivery of the aforesaid toys to the designated children of the world, through conditions of ice and snow no matter how blizzardous."

Edwin and Santa looked at each other in dismay. There it was in black and white. The award only referred to snow and ice no matter how blizzardous. No mention at all of heat no matter how blisterous, or however parching with thirst. The reindeer had an open and shut case, a dinky-dy, ridgey-didge genuine industrial grievance.

Santa and Edwin began to pace round the office in circles following each other, with Santa muttering "Think, think", but they were stumped, they couldn't think of anything.

Suddenly, the phone rang. Santa and Edwin were so deep in thought that it frightened them witless. Edwin rushed to answer it.

"Hello, North Pole Toytown, Edwin Elf speaking," said Edwin in a gloomy voice.

A faint and crackly voice sounded on the other end of the phone.

"Edwin, how's it going cousin? This is Neville the Nett-Nett calling from Australia, mate. Just calling to give you a late change in the figures for Goondiwindi and Dubbo, mate. But you don't sound too jolly Eddie. What's happening, old fellah?"

"Oh Neville, we have come up against a real problem. The reindeer are complaining about the terrible heat down-under in Australia. It looks like they will go on strike, and all the children in the world could miss out this Christmas."

"Crikey! That's real crook, brother. Hey, but wait a minute, I might have an idea."

Edwin hung anxiously on the end of the line, while he heard Neville mumbling to his fellow Nett-Netts. Santa asked what was going on, and Edwin was about to reply, when Neville came back on the line.

"Hullo, still there, brother? Righto, we reckon we could arrange a relief team for the Australian leg, mate. Could you get the reindeer to bring the kids prezzies to Hobart? I mean as far as heat goes Hobart is as cool as you will get in Australia. If you can do that, we could park the reindeer in a cool store or something, and the relief team could then fill in and do Australia."

Edwin was mightily relieved. He called Neville a life saver, and said he would call him back. Edwin put the phone down. Santa could see the relief on his Chief Elf's face, and impatiently asked for the news. Santa's face also brightened up when he heard about Neville's idea, and a bit of the redness started to come back into his cheeks.

Both Santa and Edwin immediately hurried off to meet Penny and the other reindeer.

At the Stop-Work Meeting, Santa told the reindeer he agreed the
weather conditions in Australia were bad for reindeer, and that a plan
had been thought up that meant the reindeer didn't have to go on the
Australian mainland. On hearing the plan, the reindeer were rapt. They
agreed unanimously on a return to work, and Christmas was back on
track again.

The next night was Christmas Eve. Santa and his sled, towed by the
now very happy reindeer, took off from the North Pole. They circled up
high in the sky, blipped magically into something like hyperspace, then
instantly reappeared approaching New Zealand. It didn't take that long
at all for Santa to deliver presents to all the Kiwi kids. Santa is able to do
this job so quickly, that you probably couldn't even catch him on a slo-
mo replay.

Anyway, as soon as this job was done, he blipped out again, and
reappeared over Hobart. Santa's sleigh came in for a secret landing at a
bush park picked out by Neville. It was a warm night, but not too bad
for reindeer. Santa unharnessed the reindeer and looked around,
muttering to himself.

"I'm sure this was the spot. Oh, I hope nothing has gone wrong with
the plan."

Santa shook his head with worry, turned around, and tripped over Neville. The little Nett-Nett had just magically appeared right behind Santa, in his moonlit shadow.

Santa sprawled on top of Neville, nearly squashing him, and Neville complained loudly.

"Ah, fair go Santa, fair crack of the whip!"

Four of Neville's fellow Nett-Netts also magically appeared and helped Santa unsteadily back to his feet. Santa apologised to Neville while Angie, Bindi, Jimmy, and Katie dusted him off.

Neville saw Santa looking nervously around and a cheeky grin spread over his face.

"Don't worry boss, everything is under control. We've got a truck driver with a refrigerated van, who mysteriously got lost and now he is very tired and sleeping in his van behind those trees. We can put the reindeer in the van for a couple hours, no probs."

"But what about the relief team?" asked a still worried Santa.

With that, Neville put his fingers in his mouth and gave a sharp whistle. Immediately three huge red kangaroos came bounding out from the bushes and stopped in front of Santa.

"Santa, mate, I'd like to introduce you to Bouncer, Bounder, and Bonzer, three big Reds from Central Australia. Guaranteed to do the work of any six reindeer regardless of heat, and won't even need to stop for a drink."

Santa pumped Neville's hand in gratitude, while the other four Nett-Netts harnessed up the kangaroos. Once that was done, the Nett-Netts gathered around and Angie magically produced a parcel for Santa.

"It's going to be real hot work if you stay in that red boiler suit and gumboots, so we brought you a change of clothes for down-under. You can change behind that bush over there."

Santa thanked Angie and the others, went behind the bush and changed. When he emerged, the five Nett-Netts gave him a clap. Santa bowed and turned around to show off his new attire. Bush hat, Hawaiian shirt, Bermuda shorts, and, of course, thongs.

Santa again in turn pumped the hands of the five Nett-Netts. He walked around the big Reds, sprinkling pixie dust on them. Then he climbed aboard.

"Well, time is a-wasting. Got a lot to do tonight. See all you Nett-Netts shortly. Up Dancer . . . Oops, sorry. Up Bouncer, up Bounder, up Bonzer."

The big red kangaroos immediately leaped into the night sky with such a lurch, that Santa fell back onto his bag. With his thonged feet sticking straight up, and holding onto his bush hat with one hand, Santa cheerily ho-ho-ho'd like he hadn't done for quite a while.

As Santa and his Australian relief team disappeared up into the night sky, the Nett-Netts grinned mischieviously, gave each other some all around high fives, and congratulated themselves on a job well done.

"Well, it was a narrow squeak folks, but we saved Christmas. I hope nothing like this happens again," said Neville to his mates.

But little did Neville know what was in store for next year.

HOW THE B.L.F. TRIED TO WRECK CHRISTMAS

In this world, there are two forces. The force for good, and the force for bad.

One of the best forces for good is the Christmas Spirit. It is a spirit of friendship, kindness and caring, that is protected by a special organisation of magic little folk from around the world.

You already know this organisation of good little folk is called "Elves and Little Folk International Network", or "ELFIN" for short. One of their main jobs is, of course, to keep updating Santa's lists of children to receive Christmas presents, and, in Australia, this is the job of the Nett-Netts.

But there is also another international organisation. It is an organisation of bad magic little folk. All the Goblins, Gremlins, Imps, Trolls and Mee-Mee Spirits from the countries around the world belong to this dasdardly international organisation. They call this organisation simply "Bad Little Folk".

It is well known everywhere just by its initials as the "B.L.F." and you may even have heard of it already. Your parents will certainly have heard of the BLF and can tell you that it has, in the past, caused a lot of trouble.

In Australia, the affiliated members of the BLF are the Mee-Mee Spirits. You already know about Nett-Netts, but you may not know about Mee-Mees.

Aboriginal people will quickly tell you that Mee-Mees are very nasty pieces of work.

Mee-Mees are thin and bony little beings that look more like Preying Mantises than people. They have thin and pinched-looking faces, and sparse, long wispy hair that seems to float around on the top of their heads, like threads from a broken spider's web.

Very few people actually ever get to see Mee-Mees because they don't come out much during the day. On sunny days the Mee-Mees either skulk around in the deepest darkest parts of the forest, or otherwise can magically turn themselves into wisps of mist and hide in the cracks of rocks.

The Mee-Mees like to play nasty tricks in the dark and frighten people. They hate to hear laughter and fun, and like to hear crying and sadness.

What they particularly love is to hear children crying. They will snigger and giggle fit to bust when they hear a child cry, but it's just the opposite if they hear children laughing. Then, the Mee-Mee's go into an awful rage and race away shrieking with their bony fingers in their ear-holes.

Sometimes you can tell if a Mee-Mee is around, because they have an evil touch that turns your heart cold with fright. Have you ever had a cold shiver go down your back? Well it could be a Mee-Mee.

Have you ever heard a baby cry in the middle of the night? Well it could be a Mee-Mee, because they love to poke babies in their cots and wake them up. But just remember they stay right away if you laugh at them or turn on a night light.

Because Mee-Mees are so nasty and full of spite toward children, Nett-Netts in fact spend a lot of time secretly spying on Mee-Mees from the shadows, so that the Nett-Netts can protect children from Mee-Mee mischief.

This is in fact just what Angie and Neville the Nett-Netts were doing at Christmas time only a couple of years ago. This particular day just happened to be the night before Christmas Eve. They didn't know why, but Neville and Angie had a feeling that they should check up on the Mee-Mees, and see if they were up to any of their usual funny business.

And how lucky can you be that they did check up!

The evening shadows had lengthened, and the last bit of the deep orange sun was just about to go down behind the distant hills. It was a time when Mee-Mees started to get out and about, but it was also a time when Nett-Netts could slip from shadow to shadow of the forest trees, to keep watch on the Mee-Mees.

Angie and Neville had chanced to find a group of four Mee-Mees, whispering and sneering together in evil delight. The Nett-Netts used the shadows to creep right up behind the nasty, rotten, corpse coloured little beings.

The Mee-Mees did not even suspect that the Nett-Netts could hear every word as, in turn, each of the four nasty sniggering things spoke.

"Just imagine,(hee hee hee) all the children in the world crying and having a miserable time, all on the same day."

"Fantastic, fantastic, (ah-h-ha-h-ha)"

"Yeah, yeah, (hoo-h-hoo-h-hoo) and on the one day in the year that they expect to be happy!"

"I love it, I love it! (snork) What genius thought of it anyway?"

Angie and Neville were shocked to the core. It was obvious they had stumbled across some evil plan to wreck Christmas. The two Nett-Netts waited anxiously to hear the answer to the last Mee-Mee's question.

The first Mee-Mee looked around suspiciously before answering, not realising that their sworn enemies, the Nett-Netts, were only an arm's length away.

"The American Gremlins came up with the idea at the international meeting of the BLF last month. Everybody thought it was a great idea. Seeing New Zealand was the first country on Santa's list, it was put to the Tiki people, but they chickened out. So it's up to us Mee-Mees to carry the plan out to kidnap Santa as soon as he arrives in Australia. The bug we put on the elf phone that the Nett-Netts use, has given us all the info we need."

One of the other Mee-Mees sneered about the Tiki people's refusal to be part of their evil plan.

"Ah, those backsliding lily-livered Tikis. I knew we should never have invited them to join the BLF. All they ever do is pull faces and poke out their tongues. I ask you, what did they ever do that was really nasty?"

The other Mee-Mees sniggeringly agreed that it was right, proper and fitting that the BLF had expelled those yellow-bellied, gutless and spineless Tiki splitters. And anyway, now the Mee-Mees had the chance to set their reputation as the nastiest Bad Little Folk in the whole world.

The first Mee-Mee looked around suspiciously again. The others followed suit and looked around, a couple of them actually looking right at Neville and Angie. But Nett-Netts being shadows, the Mee-Mees just looked right through them. Finally the first Mee-Mee spoke again in whispered tones.

"Look, let's not talk any more. You never know when those busybody Nett-Netts might be around. But I'm sure we would smell them if they were, they're so nice and goody-goody clean. Anyway, just remember the plan. Every available Mee-Mee has been rostered on. If we do the job right, Christmas will not only be ruined in Australia but in the rest of the world, and maybe even forever!"

The other Mee-mees gave their typical sniggering agreement, magically turned into wisps of mist, and floated away into the evening shadows.

Angie and Neville stared open mouthed at each other, incredulous at the terrible plan to kidnap Santa.

"What can we do? We can't warn Santa because the Mee-Mees have a bug on the elf line," wailed Neville in a flat panic. Angie also felt a sinking feeling of despair in her stomach, but then she had a wild idea and smacked a fist into the palm of her hand.

"Well, we will just have to go and tell him in person!"

"But we can't. There's no way we could get there in time!"

"Oh yes there is. You know how big and fat Santa is? He throws a really decent shadow doesn't he? Well, maybe if we concentrate really hard and think of his shadow, just maybe we could do the biggest shadow jump in history!"

Neville stared in disbelief at a now excited Angie.

"Do a shadow jump all the way from Australia to the North Pole? Get real, Angie!"

Angie nodded with a huge grin at the still incredulous Neville. Then, the idea of setting some sort of a world record, together with the fact that they had a duty to try anything, convinced Neville they should give it their best shot.

"Okay, let's do it," he said excitedly.

The two Nett-Netts held each other's hands, closed their eyes, thought of Santa's shadow, counted to three, and gave their heads a little nod as Nett-Netts do when they shadow-jump.

The next instant, Neville and Angie found themselves flat on their backs in a dark cramped space.

"Ah, crikey!" exclaimed Neville as he squirmed round in fright.

"Yukai!" said Angie using the Aboriginal word for ouch, as Neville accidentally elbowed her in the skull.

"What's going on? Who is that under my bed?" came a voice from above as a light was switched on.

Angie and Neville crawled out from under the bed, while a surprised Santa dressed in red spotted pyjamas, stared at them.

"Well, bless my soul! Neville! Angie! How did you get under my bed? What on earth are you doing here anyway?"

Angie waved her hands excitedly as the Nett-Netts clambered to their feet.

"No time for details, Santa. We have just uncovered a plot by the BLF to wreck Christmas. The Mee-Mees plan to kidnap you when you arrive in Australia!"

"Goodness gracious me!" Santa exclaimed, and at that moment an alarmed Edwin Elf burst in the door.

"Santa, are you alright! I heard all this yelling and thumping . . . Oh, Angie! Neville! Heavens to Murgetroid, what are you doing here?" Quickly, the Nett-Netts filled Edwin in, and the four of them puzzled about what to do. By now, Santa was over the surprise of it all, and his old brain began to tick.

"Hmmm, we have to find out more about their actual plan, if we can. Our best bet might be if we could contact the Tiki people. I mean, it is to their credit that they refused to take part in the plan, and they have been expelled from the BLF, so they might be willing to help."

Edwin shook his head worriedly.

"Yes, but the trouble is, Santa, that the Tikis are not on the elf phone system, and we don't have any ELFIN agents in New Zealand that could make contact quickly."

Neville glanced at Angie, and it was obvious that they had the same thought, so Neville spoke up.

"Hey Santa, Edwin, we could be your agents. We made it with the biggest shadow jump in history to get here, so getting to New Zealand will be a cinch. All we have to have is a mental picture of where we are supposed to go."

"By golly gosh, I think I might have just the thing," said Edwin, raising a finger as a thought struck him.

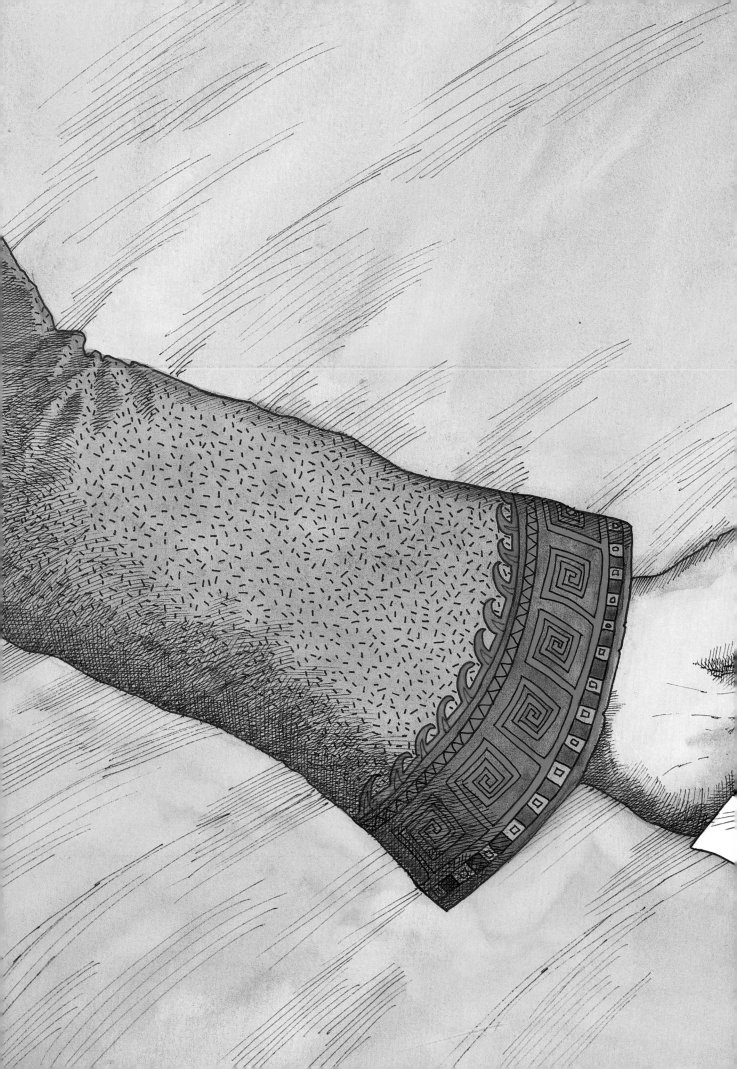

He then scuttled off out the door and back to his office, while the others looked at each other in puzzlement. Edwin was back in a flash with a photograph, which he showed to the others.

"Tikis love doing Haka war dances around their totem poles, and I just happened to take this photo when the wife and I were on an Elf Safari tour a few years back. This is a photo of Tiki headquarters, see how that totem pole casts a real good shadow?"

Angie and Neville were rapt, and reckoned it was just what they needed. They held hands, concentrated, and instantly disappeared.

For more than an hour, Father Christmas and Edwin Elf paced round the room, muttering and clicking their tongues. Time seemed to absolutely drag by. The ticking of the clock even seemed to be slower than normal. They felt helpless. If only they could hear some news.

Suddenly, there was the relief of hearing a scuffling under the bed, and out crawled Angie and Neville.

"Wow, that was a hairy experience!" announced Neville.

"Yeah, we thought the Tikis were going to barbeque us for a while," said Angie, "But since they've been expelled from the BLF they didn't mind talking. Basically, the Mee-Mees' plan is to kidnap you when you land in Hobart to use the relief team of Big Red Kangaroos."

"But we've thought of a plan that might just stop them," added Neville. "Only it will mean a fair bit of work to be done in the Elf workshop to modify Santa's sled."

"Anything at all that you need is yours. Edwin, can you take them to the workshop and get things going right away? You can fill me in on the details later!" Santa replied with an urgent sweep of his arm.

Without a moment's delay, Edwin took the Nett-Netts to the magic workshop. They explained to the Elf workers what they wanted, and drew some rough plans. The Elf workers then set to work at a frantic pace. Measuring, sawing, hammering, screwing, welding, checking plans, fetching tools and running this way and that.

While Angie kept an eye on things at the workshop, Neville shadow-jumped all the way back to Australia to give the other Nett-Netts special instructions. Within half an hour he was back again to watch the feverishly working Elves, as they now bolted the special equipment onto Santa's sleigh.

By take-off time on Christmas Eve, all was ready. There stood Santa's sled, with a big drum-like object mounted on the back. Out of the drum came a big hose that connected to a smaller drum that read "Super-Sucka, the Industrial Strength Vacuum Cleaner". Four steel rods stood on each corner of the sled, and on each rod a spotlight was mounted. Wires connected each light by a big switch, to a huge battery on the floor of the sled.

Normally the Elves were happy and noisy as they waved goodbye to Santa on this one special night of the year, but not this time. Now there were only glum and serious faces as the reindeer magically lifted off, with their noses snorting steam into the cold arctic air.

Tonight there was no parting Ho-Ho-Ho from a joyful Santa. Tonight, with Neville and Angie also on board, they were off to confront danger.

High over the North Pole, Santa pressed his special button. The sled blipped into hyperspace and instantly reappeared over New Zealand.

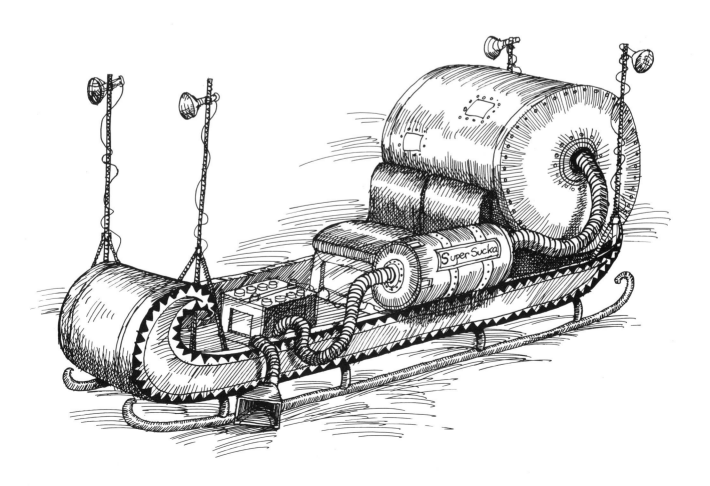

Angie and Neville really enjoyed helping Santa deliver the presents to all the Kiwi kids, and almost forgot about the danger that was ahead of them.

Soon, New Zealand was done, and with another blip, the sled magically appeared in the night sky over Hobart. With hearts beating fast, they circled in for a landing at the field where it was planned to change over the reindeer for the Big Red Kangaroos.

Neville peered down over the edge of the sled, his eyebrows knitted with worry.

"There seems to be a fair bit of mist down amongst the trees. Is the equipment ready, Angie?"

Angie patted the big drum, checked the wires leading to the switch, and replied confidently as the sled glided in to land.

"Everything is A-okay and ready to go, Nev."

It was eerily quiet as Angie spoke. Not a breath of wind or sound of a nightbird. As Santa and his two special helpers sat in the sled waiting, all they could hear was their own beating hearts.

The mist seemed strangely to be closing in toward them, as they sat in the middle of the park. It was wisping and drifting ever closer, in a way that would chill your very bones.

The reindeer started to move restlessly. Santa nervously cleared his throat.

The Nett-Netts fidgetted as the mist finally surrounded them. Somehow, there seemed to be faint sounds of evil chuckling all around.

"Now!" shouted Neville, and Angie threw the switch to the battery.

Instantly, the spotlights beamed out into the surrounding mist, and a whining noise sounded as the vacuum cleaner started up. Neville stood and held up the nozzle of the loudly sucking vacuum cleaner. Bits of mist began to be sucked into it, making strange moaning sounds. At the same time, the spotlights seemed to make the mist swirl madly away.

The spotlight had also thrown deep shadows behind the trees around the edge of the park, and from those shadows now came more than a hundred torchlights, in a circle around the park.

"You beauty, what a ripper!" exclaimed Angie, and she immediately turned off the spotlights.

When that happened, the wisps of mist began swirling away from the circle of torchlights, back toward the centre of the field. Neville, meanwhile,continued to suck up the mist with the vacuum cleaner, as it swirled helplessly toward him. In no time, every last bit of mist had been sucked into the big tank, and the circle of Nett-Netts turned off their torches.

"Worked like a charm, cousin," said a beaming Katie.

"Yeah, when you turned on the spotlights, we were able to shadow-jump to the park with our torches, easy as pie," added Jimmy.

Angie patted the big drum which seemed to be giving out muffled groans and complaints, and declared that not one Mee-Mee had escaped the Super-Sucka.

With that, the big crowd of Nett-Netts cheered. Santa removed his red hat, wiped his brow with his sleeve, and let out a big sigh of relief. He thankfully changed into his special Aussie gear once more while the Nett-Netts unharnessed the reindeer, and replaced them with kangaroos.

They also unbolted all the now unnecessary equipment, and just to make sure that Santa's sled was purified of any trace of evil from the Mee-Mees, the Nett-Netts carefully brushed it down with gum leaves. Finally, the Nett-Netts decorated the sled with all sorts of native bottlebrushes, grevilleas, and gumnuts. The magic little folk all beamed with pleasure at their dinkum Aussie Christmas decorations, and Santa gratefully thanked and shook each one by the hand, before climbing aboard.

It was a mightily relieved Santa who at last Ho-Ho-Ho'd his way up into the night sky to deliver presents to the kids of the world, without any more fear of the BLF and their evil plan.

It was a mightily relieved Santa who at last Ho-Ho-Ho'd his way up into the night sky to deliver presents to the kids of the world, without any more fear of the BLF and their evil plan.